SIX WORD STORIES

A NEW COLLECTION OF SIX WORD WONDERS

DOUG WELLER

Praise for previous releases, Six Word Wonder and Six Word Story

"This book should be a required course that you must pass before you can publish a book!"

Steve Martinson

"...a welcome diversion from real life. 5 stars!"

Diane Hernadez

"A great gift idea for anyone who appreciates words."

Charles Swanson

"I loved this book! Once I started it, I did not stop reading until I was finished except to copy some of the stories into my planner."

Donna Boyd

"Some of these little gems were laugh out loud funny, some were heartbreakingly sad, some just sort of silly, and some thought-provoking."

Carol Custer

"I am impressed! I didn't think it was possible to fit an entire story into six words, let alone over 500 of them."

Cristie Underwood

"A superbly written book that had me mesmerised... If you love reading and words, then grab this little gem up as it's amazing."

Sharon Reif

"Doug Weller delivers a host of fun, horrifying, and sometimes downright bizarre stories in Six Word Wonder!"

Joshua Grant

To be, or not to be

William Shakespeare

For the people who get it

WHAT IS A SIX WORD WONDER?

Definition of "wonder"
Noun: ...something strange or surprising
Verb: ...to think or be curious about
(dictionary.com)

Definition of a Six Word Wonder

A story, memoir, poem, or joke,
told in only six words.

WELCOME FRIEND, PLEASE LOCK THE DOOR

Six words to tell a story,
Not five, or eight, or twenty.
You may ask, is six enough?
Well, trust me, six is plenty.

If this is your first exploration into the curious world of the Six Word Wonder, then welcome. If you've already explored our previous collections, like Six Word Wonder and Six Word Story, welcome back. I missed you.

In the following pages, you will find a collection of stories, memoirs, poems, and jokes; each intended to spark a moment of intrigue, excitement, or amusement, each written in only six words.

Like a painter constrained by their canvass, a fixed allotment of six words offers a tight framework for strange, surprising, and entertaining moments. In a world where so many of us are short on time but crave stories, Six Word Wonders are a quick fix to get you through a frantic day.

In this book, you will find stories selected from over 3300 entries to the Six Word Wonder contest, alongside some of my own new writing. And later you will find the Finalists and Winner of the contest.

The stories are spread out over nine sections, with an intermission half-way through. They can be read in any order - ideal for dipping-in and flicking through. But a word of warning: I'm reliably informed that binging on too many little stories in one sitting can cause a bit of mental indigestion. Please take as many breaks as you need!

As well as enjoying these tiny wonders, I sincerely hope you are inspired to pick up a pen, or reach for a keyboard, and write some six word stories of your own. Writing miniature masterpieces is a wonderful way to stretch your creativity whatever your age or experience. To that end, the second half of this book includes a workbook filled with practical steps and exercises you can take to develop your own stories, memoirs, poems, and jokes.

Lastly, if after reading through these nuggets you do feel inspired to create, why not enter the next Six Word Wonder contest? You may even be featured in a future edition of this series. Details can be found at the back of this book.

For now, put your feet up, relax, and enjoy some six word wonders.

Doug Weller

Los Angeles

THE FIRST MOVEMENT

Newborn's first words... "Please, not again!"

Homework late.
Dog hungry.
Plan emerges.

That one thing flat-earthers fear:
Sphere.

Arrived with flowers. Left with bruises.

Scuba-diving.
Lost!
suffocating
Mermaids!
Never resurfaced.

Heaven closed:
Irretrievable lack of supply.

Introverted vampire: sucks his own blood.

Fell asleep old. Woke up cold.

Answered phone.
Stranger's voice.
Upstairs quiet.

God reset Earth to factory settings.

Biggest achievement after holidays -
remembering password!

Cannibal dated vegan.
Discovered nut allergy.

Unexpected crash
silenced
the backseat driver.

Mind rejected body.
Accepted surgeon's scalpel.

Closed eyes.
Waited 'till morning. . .
Sunrise.

Picking mushrooms. *curious* Peculiar taste.
Maaaggiiiiiiiiiiccccccc...

Missed the boat.
Hit the swimmer.

Ashley became neat pile of ashes.

Plastic flowers.
Artificial grass.
Motionless puppy.

Read this... die six days later.

Bought home.
Filled it.
Now, empty.

Buried pet.
Grieving.
Outside, there's scratching.

Remain calm. The engines have stalled.

With chilled breath, Death called me.

Left house.
Was iron unplugged?
blank

THE SECOND MOVEMENT

Missing person: last seen aiding magician.

Krash Blamdicute, United States

Dinner for two, widow and memories.

Samuel Chrapot, Australia

January dry, but drunk on you.

Paul Toolan

'Again?' we thought. 'Lockdown again? Again?'

Hans van Weerd, Australia

Strangers.
Friends.
Best friends.
Lovers.
Strangers.

Emily Delforce, Australia

"Scream!" I ordered.
The stars obeyed.

Ane Garalde, Canada

Divorce? I thought you'd never ask.

Michael P. Aleman, United States

The meaning of life is *illegible*

Kyriakos Chalkopoulos, Greece

An urn that small shouldn't exist.

Danielle Hall, United States

"Tastes like chicken." It was not.

Torché Johnson, United States

She awoke, screaming, inside her coffin.

Ashley Gonzales

WANTED: Family - contact orphanage.
REWARD: Me

Princes Rose Manuel, Philippines

One cell survived.
Mitosis.
Not again.

Humna Khan, Australia

"OH! So YOU'RE Death! Big fan."

Lily Murphy, Australia

Love letter.
Hidden box.
Husband's rage.

Sneha Shree Saikia, India

For Sale: Haunted mansion. Ghosts included.

Georgia Lewis, Australia

Sixtieth Anniversary. Never alone. Always lonely.

Fiona Grainger, United Kingdom

The reflection smiled, and stepped through…

Matthew Rowe, United Kingdom

Don't ask questions.
Just run.
NOW!

Jeff Kennedy, Anguilla

We dance under infinite stars. Together.

Tarrah Cheramie

A horse, in the hallway, waiting.

Jeremy Delgado, United States

My recipe.
Chocolate, sugar, tears, arsenic.

Jillian Lennon

Called the police, on the police.

Torché Johnson, United States

Only silence responded to her screams.

Skylar Peck, South Korea

Bubbles; last words reaching the surface.

John Pearce, Australia

Her disease; treatable.
Diagnosed during autopsy.

Bligh Chanan-Turner, Australia

THE THIRD MOVEMENT

We buried her.
Not deep enough.

Desirel Ng, Australia

―――――

Poisoned cup: left. No: right. Hmmm...

Richard Salsbury, United Kingdom

―――――

In youth, we briefly live forever.

Donald A. Ranard, United States

Past glories rise in quiet streets.

Brian Hall, Australia

Heart attack confirmed he has one.

Rohith Bandaratilaka, Sri Lanka

The herbalist lives on borrowed thyme.

Annmarie Ragukonis, United States

I am, I think. . . am I?

Donald W. Falconer

"I'm a liar," said the paradox.

Ebony Bell, Australia

Happiness is a puppy named Graham.

Elisa Gabrielle Donahue, United States

Life has become
masks and funerals.

Jennifer McCubbin, United States

Basement elevator attendant seeks a raise.

Philip Kingsley, United Kingdom

Wife pregnant. Husband shocked; secret vasectomy!

Philomena Daly, Ireland

The groom checked his watch, again.

Jake Findlay, United Kingdom

The cliff crumbled under her feet.

Nicky Cassar White, Malta

The Invisible Man died.
Nobody noticed.

Jude Abraham, Israel

Grief: Two place settings, one diner.

Monica Fernandez, United States

Shooting stars, wishes galore. . . none granted.

Alison McBain, United States

He gasped, then clutched his throat.

John Morris, United Kingdom

Gone fishing.
Hooked up.
Never returned.

Jules Martin, United States

He polished her skull twice daily.

Gordon Langley

Cemetery Plot for Sale... False Alarm.

Katy Deland, United States

Lock the doors before it's too—

Katy Deland, United States

Old friends share a twin bed.

Erin P McCurdy, United States

He snored. Her pillow created silence.

Petra Glover

The bagpipe bellowed. The flag folded.

Annmarie Ragukonis, United States

Zombies love brains. Hunger for knowledge?

Paul Lewthwaite, United Kingdom

Christening robe. Wedding dress. Burial shroud.

Ruth Jepson, United Kingdom

THE FOURTH MOVEMENT

Hyperventilating, overthinking, sobbing, panicking;
still alive...

Ambar Marrero, United States

―――――――

"Lights on please," the monster begged.

Leena Knell Nox, Australia

―――――――

Inscrutable cat,
please acknowledge
my stroking.

Paul Toolan

"Come with me. . . into the basement."

Thomas Stewart, United States

Then: Wow, a stick!
Now: Boredom.

Manesh Koshy George, India

The tombstone bore a name. His.

Luke Shepherd

The school burned.
Students cheered.
"Freedom!"

Mackenzie Stoudt, United States

His parrot mimics his victim's cries.

Kyla Gruta, Philippines

First date.
White jeans.
Loose bowels.

Christopher Witty, France

My life behind bars.
A landlady.

Jan Price, United Kingdom

Vows were prepared, but never spoken.

Heather Gillespie, Canada

You grew roots. I grew wings.

Xan Indigo, France

Friends fumbling.
Foetus forming.
Father fuming.

Sam Mitchell, United Kingdom

Alice: Last seen near rabbit hole.

Aliyaa Pathan, United States

Scandals are lies - truth always hides.

La-Chanda Smith, United States

The distracted chicken crosses into eternity.

Laura Beck, United States

Waited for Godot. He didn't show.

Maureen Crisp, United Kingdom

What do you mean, 'Hello dad?'

Stuart McDowall, United Kingdom

Removing her veil, she found freedom.

Diana Davison, Australia

Crisp sheets, clean bodies, dirty minds.

Tim Kirton

"Are you cheating?" asked the cheater.

Pragya P, India

Today we celebrate. Tomorrow we repent.

Jennifer Haggerty, United States

No collar,
no owner,
no future.

Petra Glover

Twenty-twenty taught us: Please unmute yourself.

Siraj Khan, United States

The shoes were all that remained.

Olivine Marie, United States

Glass half full, dropped it - damn!

Lottie Dale, United Kingdom

THE FIFTH MOVEMENT

At ventriloquist's funeral, the dummy spoke.

———

Review of critic's murder:
Thumbs up.

———

...matrix. There's a glitch in the...

———

So THAT'S what chloroform smells li–

———

My deep-fake clone
is a looker.

Erected hammock.
Gingerly mounted.
Instantly grounded.

Tigress lets her keeper move closer...

Urgently dialled 'Missing Persons'.
Nobody answered.

Virus multiplied as the country divided.

Spot the difference:
I am gone.

First test smartypants ever failed? Covid.

Perhaps dogs really want YOUR bones...

Early Americans lost their volume controls.

Behind her mask, was another mask.

Your resume...?
More like your eulogy.

Latest cure for sore throats.
Guillotine.

#metoo plus hard-drinking - became #wethree

———

Got a text!
"Mind that bus!!!"

———

Exhausted?
Pray for reincarnation as cat.

———

Snooze button upgraded!
Now induces coma.

———

Weightless. Miles from Earth. Still bored.

———

On your marks.
Get set.
Oblivion.

Something smells good!
sniffing my bloodhound

At first sunlight, goodbye to night.

Politicians lied. Blackened skies. Everyone dies.

Tooth fairy reveals truth about Santa.

Please, run. My dogs prefer hunting.

Visited flea market.
Left SO itchy!

INTERMISSION

To be, or not to be

When William Shakespeare popped this briefest of questions into Hamlet's mouth, it was surely no accident.

Six words - each as short as they could possibly be. Each so simple a child of six could repeat it. Six syllables, six beats - three short, three long.

The Great Bard is famed for his creative and expansive use of language, for his vast soliloquies featuring exotic new words, for plays that run for hours. And Hamlet is his longest play, totalling over 30,000 words from opening to curtain call.

And yet, it is this stripped-back six word question that Billy used to ask the most powerful and painful question anyone could ask of themselves.

The entire play spins on this briefest of lines. The strikingly simple words leap from the stage and into our collective consciousness.

And we recognise a question straight from the heart. A question that only time will answer. To be, or not to be, that is the question.

The power of six words can be mighty indeed, and if six words is good enough for Willy, it's good enough for me.

THE SIXTH MOVEMENT

Please stop eating your regurgitated past.

Brea Pringle, Australia

He ran into my knife. Thrice.

Alyanna Sy, Philippines

On oak tree, inscribed, love me.

Rashi Gaikwad, India

They got married.
Opposites stopped attracting.

Awneet Singh, India

And Eve took her first bite.

Emma Moisa, Netherlands

Never learned swimming.
Too late now.

Chris Clemens, Canada

Sale: Engagement ring. One careless owner.

Philip Kingsley, United Kingdom

Pursuing prestige brought him luxurious loneliness.

Summer Austin, United States

"You've gotta stop finishing my——?"
"–Sentences?"

Donald A. Ranard, United States

Henry VIII - Anne Boleyn - caught necking.

Joann Majerle, United States

I held hands with my killer.

John Pearce, Australia

He hit send,
then a tree.

Abbie Harris, United Kingdom

Midnight, Romulus. Bring more bricks tomorrow.

David Silver, United Kingdom

Flowers bloom above her buried body.

Kyla Gruta, Philippines

Wanted: Husband —
declawed, neutered, house-trained, cuddly.

Bethany Jarmul

The fight started at the funeral.

O'Neill Renton, United Kingdom

Three birds chirped,
fourth one lip-synched.

Sagar J, India

A push.
Crying eyes.
Congratulations. . . twins!

Diana Davison, Australia

"Ma'am, it's JUST a gunshot wound."

Lily Murphy, Australia

A cry in the dark.
Ceasefire.

Sam Mitchell, United Kingdom

Song.
Play.
Pause.
Cry.
Play.
Repeat.

Ian Davos, Romania

Prodigal at birth, pauper at death.

Tashi Chaturvedi, India

"To play devil's advocate. . ." said God.

Lin Let, United Kingdom

Being a cardiologist
broke his heart.

Sneha Mukherjee

Sleep peacefully, beautiful child.
Forever young.

Rebekah Lawrence, United Kingdom

Mary had a little lamb. . . Chop.

Martin Cameron, United Kingdom

THE SEVENTH MOVEMENT

She grew like roses. Resplendent. Sharp.

Xan Indigo, France

From virus to vaccine; Twenty-twenty won.

Phanindra Ivatury, Netherlands

Bouncy castle entrepreneur
demands inflated nobility.

Granville Brown, United Kingdom

I leave.
Forgot my mask.
Again!

Heather Gillespie, Canada

The identical twin was beside himself.

James A. Tweedie, United States

backwards. life your live cannot You

Leslie Roberts, United Kingdom

In the end,
there was darkness.

Jo Mularczyk, Australia

Table for three: Man, Wife, Trouble.

Miriam Ikwueme, Nigeria

"Bechdel?" she asked Meryl. "What's that?"

Tamsin Kerr, Australia

Smashed cookies.
Spilled milk.
Fallen Santa.

Jennifer Haggerty, United States

Overboard. Submerged.
Sharks bigger than expected.

Michelle Keeley, United Kingdom

Just using six words is too...

Martin Cameron, United Kingdom

Apparently, dumb duck got the quack.

Soft Remedy, Indonesia

Empty leash.
Heavy urn.
Final walk.

Casey Curtis, United States

Contemplation.
Commendation.
Then condemnation.
Rationalisation.
Hospitalisation.

L. E. Morgan, Australia

It was torture to write this.

Wendy Eisenberg, United States

Makeshift raft. Stormy seas. Angry reception.

Richard Salsbury, United Kingdom

She didn't know she'd be last.

Olivia Lindquist

Dad kept score - using the obituaries.

Julie McNeely-Kirwan, United States

———

Happiness - invention of mirrors, then sadness.

Juliana Ghetto, Australia

———

The moon yearns to kiss the sun.

Heather Wightman, United Kingdom

———

Nonsense, we are out of range. . .

Stuart McDowall, United Kingdom

———

Jumped. Then I changed my mind.

Scott Bradbrook

Lost: Myself. Please return if found.

Olivia Hartwell, United Kingdom

She departed without the hidden suitcase.

Ashley Gilland, United States

Pawn shop. Purple Heart. Never worn.

Mike Walker

Alzheimer's??? Impossible. No one told me.

Amy Cree, United States

Sows cotton. Cotton grows. Sews cotton.

Megan Oliver, Australia

Words pass. Meanings linger, like ghosts.

Xan Indigo, France

Laughing women peeled off their skin.

Dj Robbins

THE EIGHTH MOVEMENT

Paramedic's finished her text. . . 'love you.'

Emily Delforce, Australia

———

Cardboard signs say, "Save the trees."

Kyla Gruta, Philippines

———

Daddy's home! Mommy, please hide now.

Natasia Rea, United States

Beyond my depth, desperate for air.

Emma Hartley, United States

Opticians made a spectacle of themselves.

Alan Russell, United Kingdom

Turns out, her hips do lie.

James Michelle, United States

"Tiiimberrr!"
"Oh God!"
"No! No! No!"

Sean Wright, United States

She hugged me tightly. I farted.

Richard Liu, Taiwan

Illiterates could've better read the room.

Lin Let, United Kingdom

"You'll be heroes!" both sides declared.

Shaun McKenna, United Kingdom

To do: cancel wedding, hire hitman

Kiera Gracie

Got his baby.
Lost his lady.

Padma Poorani S, India

Crossing the graveyard, he felt alive.

Carmen Bock

The voice whispered, "not now dear."

Rhonda Russell

Cake sitting,
Dad missing,
police knock.

Matthew Ochrym, United States

For sale: politician's brain. Never used.

Sue Mitchell, Australia

Lost my keys, and my dignity.

Katie Ulrich, United States

The middle floorboard gave way slightly.

Jon Colman, United Kingdom

Anguished but starving,
he ate her. . .

Martha Letseka, Lesotho

Six strings,
four chords,
eyes crying.

John Pearce, Australia

Character coughs.
Dead in five, guaranteed.

Richard Salsbury, United Kingdom

In Nowhere, Arizona, iguanas wander aimlessly.

Lisa Marie Lopez

No. That's not MY missing foot.

Anna Scaife, New Zealand

Hatred.
Darkness.
Compromise.
Understanding.
Light.
Love

Clarissa Mchardy, United Kingdom

You're so sweet, but I'm diabetic.

Bradley Sancken, Japan

He removed his mask. She screamed.

Royston Ellis, Sri Lanka

Humming Happy Birthday, with soapy hands.

Angela Deane, United Kingdom

On harvest day, we had rats.

Yess Bryce

It's bewitching season, fetch the cauldron!

Alice Raison, United Kingdom

It's gone quiet in Mission Control.

Amy Cree, United States

THE NINETH MOVEMENT

Don't keep reading. I said DON'T!

Arthur's only recent house guests?
Maggots.

Immobilised.
Screaming for help.
bachelor's party

Kim's Miami vices: burgers and fries.

Called divorce hotline.
All operators engaged.

Youngest son.
Drastic action.
Became eldest.

Minutes elapsed. . .
then the supercomputer wept.

Werewolf! Where? ...wolf, yes. Wearing what?

Saves the whole universe.
Now what?

When I dream... you never feature.

Sometimes,
your beauty
makes me
breathless.

Skeleton came out of the closet.

In a thousand years, nobody cared.

"I'm starving."
"How you doin, Starving?"

Twisting the tap, the gas flowed.

Rudolph's red nose - diagnosis says malignant.

Plane crash. Sole survivor - satisfied smile.

Foolproof plan.
But, unfortunately, not Dave-proof.

First date ended
with last goodbye.

Yesterday, my burst of creativity burst.

Started last period.
Got first period.

At home.
Lights out.
Writing stories.

New clothes.
New body.
Same halitosis.

Festive cost cutting.
Elf was shelved.

And, for the appetiser? Your eyeballs.

Wanted to end,
but held on.

SIX WORD WONDER CONTEST
2022

To celebrate the launch of our last book, Six Word Story, we ran the second year of our contest to find the best new Six Word Wonder.

The contest's ambition was to encourage as many people as possible to experiment with the six word format, and hopefully discover fresh new stories, poems, memoirs, and jokes.

Your response to the contest was phenomenal.

More than 3,300 entries were submitted. Entries came from all over the world, from Australia to Zimbabwe, via Uzbekistan, Bosnia, India, and Brazil.

We saw stories of darkness and light, of amusement, and genuine seriousness. In the judging, we whittled the stories down to a shortlist for inclusion, which were then scattered through these pages. The full shortlist of names can be found at the back of this book.

A huge thank you to all who entered. If your story didn't feature, don't be disheartened. There is no rule-book for what a great Six Word Wonder is - it's just a matter of opinion and instinct. Perhaps the best response to any frustration you feel is to grab a pen and write!

Before sharing the winner, a few observations following the judging. There were a vast variety of stories, memoirs, poems, and jokes, ranging across genres from romance, to horror, right through to philosophy and politics. Current themes like the Covid-19 pandemic featured heavily, as did old favourite spins on the classic - For Sale: Baby Shoes. Never Worn.

The best Six Word Wonders made you pause for thought, triggering a true emotion. And, if you find yourself thinking of the story again and again, it's a great contender.

For those keen on creating and sharing more stories, details of the next Six Word Wonder contest are included in the back of this book.

The best examples of Six Word Wonder shared a few things in common:

- Drew a definite emotional response.
- Featured beauty, suspense, amusement, or surprise.
- Took the reader on a journey, even if they needed to fill in the blanks.
- Used only six words!

The winning entry met all these criteria. It seems simple but is truly affecting.

Before announcing the winner, here are the finalists across the four major categories of Six Word Wonder - best story, best poem, best memoir, and best joke.

THE FINALISTS

SIX WORD WONDER 2022

Nobody knew where the oceans went.

Michelle Keeley
Best Six Word Wonder - Story

She wove spells into her sweaters.

Sebya Gorre-Clancy
Best Six Word Wonder - Poem

THE FINALISTS

SIX WORD WONDER 2022

Saturday night dancing on Dad's feet.

Julie Bobzien
Best Six Word Wonder - Memoir

Our marriage couldn't survive the trombone.

Robert Carroll
Best Six Word Wonder - Joke

WINNER

SIX WORD WONDER 2022

Nobody knew where the oceans went.

Michelle Keeley, United Kingdom

SIX WORD WONDER WORKBOOK

by Doug Weller

WELCOME TO THE SIX WORD WONDER WORKBOOK

Hi

I really hope you enjoyed Six Word Stories and got a taste for the variety of effects that can be achieve in only a tiny number of words.

My hope with all the books in the Six Word Wonder series is to share the six word art form and encourage more people to pick up a pen, or reach for a keyboard, to create their own mini-masterpieces.

In this bonus section of the book, you will find a how-to guide to writing and developing more of your own six word creations. You can use it to practice the art, develop your language and creative skills, or just to have a bit of indulgent fun.

The reason I love to read and write Six Word Wonders? They let me take a brief step away from reality.

I'm entertained by a story, amused by a joke, intrigued by a memoir, or moved by a poem. And, just for a moment, all the background noise of the day ceases.

If there is one thing better than reading Six Word Wonders, it is writing them. This section is intended to complement the Six Word Wonder book series, to encourage you to go deeper, and experiment more with this format.

By the end of this workbook, I hope that you will have written many Six Word Wonders of your own. Some will be lousy, and some won't make sense.

But some... some will be brilliant!

So, get focused, get adventurous, get creative. Keep your stories short, and your ideas big.

WHO IS THIS WORKBOOK FOR?

Anybody can enjoy this workbook. Six Word Wonders are for all ages and abilities. By the end, you should have created many stories, memoirs, jokes, and poems of your own.

There are a few groups who might get particular benefits from these pages. If you don't see yourself listed here, why not scribble yourself in at the bottom?

1. Lovers of Six Word Stories. Be empowered to write your own.

2. Aspiring writers, looking to flex their creativity muscles and unearth writing prompts.

3. Students of language, wanting to explore the inner workings of words, syntax and punctation.

4. People seeking a mindful practice. Get in the flow with your compositions.

Who is this workbook not for?

This workbook will work best if you get fully interactive. Pull out a notebook and pen, and get writing. If you don't want to write your own stories, you might leave these pages feeling a little deflated.

TEN TIPS TO GET THE MOST
FROM THIS WORKBOOK

1. This workbook is **yours to play with**. It is a safe space for experimentation, creation and adventure.

2. The workbook is divided up into sections - all intended to **stimulate your ideas and thoughts.**

3. **Grab a pen, pencil, or keyboard.** Don't be afraid to scribble, scrawl, write, and sketch on a notepad or in the margins.

4. There's **no need to read the workbook in order.** Jump around as much as you like.

5. **Be creative** - there are no right or wrong answers. Only what feels right to you.

6. Initially, focus on quantity. **Write as many stories as you can.**

7. Try different styles, punctuation, genres. Experiment. **Break things!**

8. **Edit, re-edit, try different angles.** There's always a new way to approach a Six Word Wonder.

9. You don't need to read any other books from the Six Word Wonder series in order to benefit from this workbook. But the more micro-fictions you've read, the more new ideas you might have. . .

10. Everything here is intended to stimulate you to write your own stories, poems, jokes and memoirs. **Get writing!**

I hope you're excited. Let's begin.

SIX REASONS TO WRITE SIX WORD WONDERS

Therapy - writing is soothing and mindful.

Craft - tight stories need authorial skill.

Practicing brevity - keep it simple, stupid.

Refining arguments - reword until it's perfect.

Core language skills - dictionary, thesaurus, research.

Health - we're all addicted to passivity.

FIRST, WRITE SIX WORDS

Before we go any further, I want you to write a Six Word Wonder.

For some readers, this will be your first ever six word utterance. For others, you may have written many before. It doesn't matter.

Why write a story so soon?

1. Get practical now. **This is a workbook.** That means a little work from you.

2. Break any barriers that lead to over-thinking. **Take action.**

3. Recognise **there are no "wrong" or "bad" six word wonders.**

4. Creation is the goal, first and foremost.

So pull out a pen. Go ahead. Just write six words:

Feeling good?
Hungry to spill more words?
Great.

Maybe your creative juices are already flowing. Awesome.

If you already have some Six Word Wonders desperate to escape from your head, you can release them here and put them on the page.

Don't worry, nobody is watching!

If you filled a page, fantastic! Now, let's learn about the six common forms of Six Word Wonder.

COMMON FORMS OF SIX WORD WONDER

There are many forms of Six Word Wonder. In the next pages, we are going to learn a bit more about certain types of Wonder. You will also have a chance to experiment with each type as we go. Six Word Wonders can be funny, serious, light, dark, playful, poetic, absurd, or any combination of these.

Common Forms of Six Word Wonder:

Six Word Stories

Here, you try to tell a narrative in six words, with a beginning, middle and an end.

Six Word Jokes

The focus of a Six Word Joke is to deliver a laugh (or a groan) from your reader. They are meant to be amusing, droll, sarcastic or cheeky.

Six Word Poetry

Six Word Poems are intended to evoke emotion through the power of language.

Six Word Memoirs

Memoirs are autobiographical. They are a tiny summary of the person you are, inside or out. Writing on your tombstone is optional.

Six Word Advice

Capture an astute piece of advice in only six words.

Six Word Riddles

In a Six Word Riddle, you play with language, format and word order to set up a short riddle or puzzle for the reader to solve within the words.

SIX WORD STORIES

Storytelling is a deep, human drive. We crave narrative, and instinctively create stories to understand the world around us. Telling a story in only six words is a particular challenge.

You are ideally trying to find **a beginning, a middle, and an end.**

Or, you could think of it like a magic trick. The Pledge, the turn, and the Prestige.

These elements are the scaffolding, or **framework that holds your story structure in place.** You may not find all these elements immediately obvious when reading six word stories. Sometimes, that's because they are not there. At other times, it's because they are craftily hidden.

When you are writing your stories, whether they are six words or sixty-thousand words, think about how you've applied the core elements of storytelling.

Here are five questions to ask as you try to create six word stories:

- Do you have characters/protagonists/antagonists?
- Do you have a setting?
- Do you have a plot? Does something happen?
- Do you have conflict or drama?
- Do you reach a resolution of some kind?

Think of a story you know well, like a favourite book or movie. I bet you can name all the questions above for that story. So why not for a story you are writing yourself?

ELEMENTS OF A SIX WORD WONDER

Let's use the most famous six word wonder of all to test the story criteria.

For Sale: Baby Shoes. Never worn.

Protagonist
The person selling the baby shoes.

Setting
Newspaper advertisement. But we imagine the protagonist writing the words.

Plot
A parent is choosing/forced to sell shoes that their baby never got the chance to wear.

Conflict or Drama

The conflict is between the cute thought of baby shoes, to the tragedy of them not being worn.

Resolution

You are left with tragic emptiness.

Now, use what you've learned to **write some narrative stories.** Who are your characters? What's the situation? What's the conflict or drama? And, what's the resolution?

Don't worry if you haven't painted every detail. You only have six words.

Your reader will fill in the blanks.

SIX WORD JOKES

Jokes, rib-ticklers, quips and witticisms - however you describe them, **six words are surprisingly versatile vehicles for delivering jokes.** Some will make you groan. Some will make you nod in appreciation of the construction.

Occasionally, they might even make you laugh!

Most six word jokes have some kind of a set-up and a punchline. Indeed, many more serious Six Word Wonders also follow a similar format: a set-up, followed by a surprise. The only thing really dividing the jokes from the tragedies is what exactly the surprise contains.

The standard format for a joke requires a set-up to give the reader an expectation. You read the words and in your head it paints a particular picture. The punchline subverts this expectation. The words are not what you expect, and the new angle or twist breaks you out of your preconceived idea.

Here are a few examples of set-ups and punchlines to help illustrate how this structure works. (P.S. I can't promise that you will find these funny, but hopefully, you will appreciate the structure so you can apply it to your own work.)

Stole her diary.
Got twelve months.

Time travel is possible. . .
Just wait!

Sued the airline.
Lost my case.

Several standard frameworks for jokes exist for you to experiment with. They are useful for helping you think about how you structure any Six Word Wonder. Of course, these structures work whether you are writing a six word joke, or a joke of any length.

Six Word Jokes could be simple one-liners, or may be observational, personal (self-deprecation), topical, or satirical.

On the previous page, we talked about Setup and Punchline. There are many other structures that stem from this. Here's a few examples:

Double set-up

The next is to add in more than one set up, essentially creating a list of ordinary sounding things, then end with a zinger. Something random or surprising.

This could be: Set up. Set up. Strange/Shocking/Unexpected.

Met girl.
Married her.
Sobered up.

Simile

With a simile, you are comparing something to something else, sometimes using a "like" or an "as if." The simile is generally an odd juxtaposition.

He reminds me of Churchill...
Chubby.

Familiar phrases twisted

Take a well-known phrase or idiom and twist it somehow. The punchline is the surprise from the twist. This often works best for a local audience. For example, who doesn't love this Led Zeppelin song?

She's buying a stairlift to heaven.

Puns

With puns the punchline, or somewhere in the set up, has a double meaning. And the twist of the meaning is what brings the surprise. Puns, using words with double meanings, homonyms and homophones. For example, the word intense and the phrase 'in tents', could lead to:

Went camping during earthquake... In tents.

Look for words with double meanings. Create a Six Word Wonder with one of them.

For example, let's take the word Beef. The word is a type of cow meat, and also a type of complaint.

Remember to save the punchline for the end.

Bull got upset with menu. Beef!

Failed to laugh?
Test your pulse.

Over to you - use a notepad to try out all the styles of a Six Word Joke. As a recap, some of the main structures for Six Word Jokes are:

- Set-up and punchline
- Double set-up
- Simile
- Familiar phrase twisted
- Puns

SIX WORD MEMOIRS

Six Word Memoirs are personal autobiographies written in only six words. You can think of them as a way to summarise your reputation, aspiration or obituary.

How would you sum up yourself in only six words?

Here's a few questions to help you think:

What are you famous for amongst your friends and family?

What do you dream of achieving in your life?

What's been the best moment of your life so far?

What would you like to be remembered for?

Which part of your personality makes you you?

Use the answers to your probing questions to improvise possible stories that are unique to you.

Now, it's your turn. **Use your probing questions**, but don't feel restricted by them. Write several memoirs that draw from your life, your experiences, and dreams for the future.

SIX WORD POETRY

Six words can be used to manipulate language to create statements of beauty and truth. Use poetry to make a powerful statement through the use of elegant and stimulating words. Try to elicit emotion and ideas.

Unlike a story, the focus here is less on the narrative, and more on the emotion contained within six words.

Like any poem, the mood is often romantic. **Use six words to share your feelings of love, trust and honor.** Be playful and reach deep inside yourself.

Without you, I am barely me.

Your lips
are shaped like kisses.

There was no music until you.

You may also use poetry to expose the darker side of emotion - the sadness and pain.

After fighting, I need you more.

I can no longer remember you.

Only through dying can we live.

Try to touch into the heart of humanity. And don't worry, your poems don't have to rhyme.

Try various different techniques of poetry to enhance and create new Six Word Poems. Here's a few elements for you to try:

Onomatopoeia
Words that imitate the sound they describe.

Alliteration
Multiple words with the same opening letter or sound.

Rhythm and Meter
An artful series of emphasised and modest words or syllable beats.

Visual Presentation
Using the words themselves to paint a shape.

Rhyming
Words that sound alike, either perfectly rhyme or slanted.

Metaphor and Simile
Using one object to describe another.

Haiku
Write six words in a five syllable, seven syllable, five syllable form.

Now, over to you.

Try out some of the different forms of poetry, or create your own.

Try to focus on the emotion you are trying evoke with your words.

SIX WORD RIDDLES

Six words can be used for word-play, puzzles, riddles, and acrostics. Here are different examples of how to play with six words.

Puzzle

Six words that set a puzzle within the words.

Example:

You complete me, said the emu.

Acrostic

First letter of each word spells another six letter word.

Example:

After
Dinner,
Usually
Like
To
Sleep.

Mirror-image

Three words, then those three words in reverse

Example:

Man wanted it, it wanted man.

Repeats

The same words or similar words repeated.

Example:

The cow heard the cow herd.

Consistent word length

Every word is the same number of letters. E.g. all two letters

Example:

An ax
to do
my ox.

Initialism

Sentences written using letter only

Example:

'U C A B?'
'I C.'

Loops

The sentence can be read over and over.

Example:

...ended. The day started as it...

Now **create your own Six Word Riddles.**

Can you complete all the different styles?

SIX WORD ADVICE

Six words can impart a great deal of information. Life insights to be passed from one person to the next.

Examples of Six Word Advice

Always check
behind closed shower curtains.

———

Chances are,
your instincts are wrong.

———

When someone offers toothpaste,
accept it.

Keep calm
and don't carry on.

Monday?
It's Sunday minus the hope.

Now, try writing some Six Word Advice of your own.

SIX WORD HISTORY

In Six Word History, you pick a real or mythical incident, or person from history and try to sum it up in six words. It's a bit like a memoir, but rather than being about yourself or someone you know, it is about a person or an event from history.

Here are some examples. I've added titles to help you place the person or event. Of course, your wonder should make sense without the title!

Vincent Van Gogh

Painted sunflowers. Severed ear. Died alone.

The First World War

Thousands at the trenches.
Few returned.

Princess Diana

Divorced princess lived happily never after.

The Ending of the Second World War

Normandy landings.
Got lucky.
Liberated France.

SIX WORD JOBS

Pick a job - a person's employment. Come up with a smart, silly, or amusing story about their life, then sum it up in six words.

Here are some examples:

At the wedding,
the photographer snapped.

Yesterday, they dug up an archeologist.

Statistician miscalculated his chance of survival.

Air traffic controller's last day?
Impactful.

With an almost limitless supply of different jobs,
you could be composing these stories all day.

SIX WORD WONDER - ALPHABET PEOPLE

Here's a challenge. Write an alliterative six word wonder about a friend, neighbour or imaginary character. Every word starts with the same letter.

A few examples of Six Word Wonder - Alphabet People:

Angry Albert arranged another angling accident.

Devilish Doug decisively defeated demented Darren.

Joyless Jonathan just joined jealous jobless.

Noble Noah neglected naive non-believers notifications.

Pretty Penelope, predictably, piled on pounds.

RULES FOR WRITING SIX WORD WONDERS

Of course, any creative writing is far more about creation than it is about rules.

But... there are a few guidelines which should help keep everything consistent and orderly.

Remember, a painter is restricted by the size of their canvas, and a composer is restricted by octaves.

Think of these limits as actually helping creativity by preventing the dreaded blank page.

- Each Six Word Wonder consists of **six words**. No more, no less.
- **Titles are included** in word count.
- **Contractions allowed**: It's for it is.

- **Unlimited punctation** can be used achieve the best effect.
- **Hyphenated words:** can be one or two words depending on context

TIPS FOR IMPROVING YOUR SIX WORD WONDERS

- Use only six words!
- Use **punctuation** to enhance your meaning.
- Aim for **beginning, middle, and end**.
- **Spark an emotion**, suspense, or surprise.
- Many stories benefit from **a twist or punchline**
- **Strong verbs** produce much stronger stories.
- **Mold ideas** until the shape fits.
- Share your work - **listen to feedback.**
- **Have fun** - rules can be broken.

Next, we will explore some of the ways to use grammar to get the most out of your stories.

SIX WORD GENRES

Six Word Wonders can be in any genres. Here's a bunch of Six Word Wonders, split by genre to help illustrate the point. Once you learn how to recognise the genre, you can intentionally write in one style or another.

Romance
Eight billion people.
You chose me.

Horror
Hugged her 'til her bones cracked.

Comedy

Wanted: Web developer. Preferably a spider.

Science-Fiction

God checks manual.

Orders a reboot.

Fantasy

Entered cave. Defeated dragon. No treasure!

Mystery / Thriller

Ace.

King.

Queen.

Jack.

Three.

Damn!

War

Appeasement failed. Bomb dropped. Peace restored.

Biography

Casting couch.
Stray hands.
Life imprisonment.

Literary

My heart didn't break. . . It shattered.

POWER VERBS

Verbs drive action within stories.

Strong and powerful verbs are the most active and interesting choices.Cross off weak verbs and experiment with strong verbs.

State of being verbs like **Be; Is; Am** are weak. Where possible, replace them with stronger verbs. 'Ing' verbs like walking, drinking, smiling could also be considered weak.

Verbs needing adverbs (words ending in 'ly') are often weak. Try **'gulped'** instead of **'swallowed nervously'**, and **'stared'** instead of **'watched intensely'**.

Example of how to use Power Verbs in a Six Word Story:

Clare **looked** at her love rival.

See how the meaning changes and becomes more specific with each alternative word for the verb. Each alternative creates an entirely different story.

Clare **glared** at her husband's colleague.
Clare **admired** her husband's colleague.
Clare **peeked** at her husband's colleague.
Clare **inspected** her husband's colleague.

Which verb made most of an impact for you? Why?

There are hundreds more powerful verbs to play with. **Use dictionaries, thesaurus and power verb lists** to get more inspiration.

Now, pick a verb or two and experiment by creating a story and then **switching around the verbs.**

CURIOUS NOUNS

Nouns are the objects in your story. Most stories will feature a noun of some kind. Every noun, abstract or real, has its own meaning, emotions and textures attached to it.

Once you choose a noun, a story might fall out. For example, once you have decided your story will feature the noun 'Bed', you might get:

Bed springs creak above my head.

or

Woke in bed. A flower bed.

Or how about 'cat'?

Cat, on ninth life, risks jump.

or

Lost: Cat. Reward: If stays lost.

Every noun, every object has thousands of possible stories associated with it. Your job is to **choose the noun and then chisel out the story.**

Now, do some noun and verb combinations.

Try to get power out of the verbs and curiosity from the nouns.

PLAYING WITH PUNCTUATION

Punctuation can be used to **highlight, alter tempo, and improve understanding.** Experiment with different punctuation marks.

Here are some examples of how punctation can drive stories to new heights.

Punctuation Type

Exclamation mark !

Call an ambulance. This'll be quick!

Question mark ?

Virus that eventually ends us? Mankind.

Ellipses . . .

... mind. Gifted Mediums can read your...

Comma ,

Honestly, I accidentally sat on it.

Speech marks " or '

'Wouldn't harm fly,' claims reformed spider.

CAPITALISE'
What d'ya mean? I'M NOT SHOUTING!'

Italics

It's not *my* fault you're extinct.

Emphasis *

In bed. Almost asleep. *hears breathing*

Line
spacing

He learned
to love
too late.

And the rest &, $, %, [,], ;, :,

For sale: Clown shoes. Never fit.

ELIMINATE WASTED WORDS

You only have six words - so make every word count. **Cut out any word that's not vital for the story's meaning.**

Words you can often edit out include:

The. I. You. They. Be. Is. A. Just. Really.

Below, you can see a set of story examples. In each wonder, there are one or more wasted words. Use a pen, or in your head, cross out the wasted words until you have uncovered a Six Word Wonder.

The podiatrist sure loved the smell of feet.

Finally, I had enough time.
I finished everything.

It is only her son who still remembers her.

The wedding resumed, this time without the groom.

Sleeping cat? Really? Hasn't moved in weeks.

Invisible man crouched down
close beside her.

SIX WORD WONDER FORMATS

You can use also use certain formats or frameworks for your story to stimulate more ideas.

Here are a few examples of formats you can build on. Each one includes an example to help with your understanding.

Format: For Sale: [Object] [Circumstance]

Example: For Sale: Open parachute. Strings cut.

Format: Wanted: [Object] [Detailed requirement]

Example: Wanted: Murderer who killed my inspiration

Format: Secret: [Tell us a secret]
Example: Secret: I'm the saddest funny person.

Format: [Something honest sounding], she/he/name lied.

Example: I'm telling the truth, she lied.

Format: Lost/Found: [A thing] Found/Lost: [An surprising/emotional thing]

Example: Lost: Magic Beans. Found: Giant Beanstalk.

REVISION AND SELF EDITING

So far, we have been all about open creativity. Just writing and playing with whatever comes to mind. But to really refine and perfect your Six Word Wonders, you need to give them a proper edit.

Here you can use all you've learned about structure, genre, punctuation, power verbs and curious nouns. Put it all together to turn your stories into the best version of themselves.

To help you better understand the editing process, here is a real-life example of my edit process for a particular story that featured in Six Word Wonder.

It all starts with an idea. I had a spark of inspiration for a story about a doctor arriving at a house too late to help somebody in need. A really sad little moment, that probably happens every day. Next, I jotted down a possible story:

> The doctor arrived after the accident.

That's a basic story. My challenge is then to tighten it. First, I tried a few alternatives for the subject.

> The medics arrived after the accident.
> The helicopter arrived after the accident.
> The ambulance arrived after the accident.

I liked the drama of an ambulance arriving, picturing the drama of a quiet street being disturbed by the siren.

Next, I looked at the incident, ramping up the seriousness of the event.

> The ambulance arrived after the disaster.
> The ambulance arrived after the fire.
> The ambulance arrived after the heart-attack.

There's two wasted words to cut.

> Ambulance arrived after the heart-attack.

There's a lot of "A" alliteration (repeated letters in

this one) - perhaps too much. Now, to play with word order.

The heart-attack arrived before the ambulance.

First, a heart-attack, then, an ambulance.

Finally, the ambulance arrived. No siren required.

Then, try two sentences, to get to the final story as published.

Ambulance finally arrived. Left without siren.

Is this story perfect? No. Does it give me pause to think and fire a dark emotion when I read it? I went through multiple iterations of language, syntax, and specifics before getting to a story I was happy with. But the basic story still holds the essence of my original idea.

A Six Word Wonder is never finished. There is always room for improvement.

WRITING EXERCISES USING SIX WORD WONDERS

You can use Six Word Wonder for all kinds of writing exercises to spark curiosity, ideas, and inspiration.

Opening Line

Take a Six Word Wonder as the opening line for a longer story as a writing prompt. The restriction of only six words means there is so much more that could be said. Ask questions regarding what has really happened here.

So why not say it? For example, take this as an opener:

"Unlocking the cage, she stepped out."

Who is she? Why was she in a cage? How did she unlock the cage? Where is she? Who locked her inside? Where does she go now she's out?

Rewrites and adaption

Take a Six Word Wonder and chop it up, write it from different angles, cut words, add words, change the order, change the protagonist, change the verbs, change the nouns. Use one story as a springboard for more.

Stream of consciousness

Simply choose an opening word and write.

Fake memoir

Pick a name, ask yourself the questions from the Six Word Memoir section of this workbook. Make up your own memoir for this invented person. Who could they be? A clown? A president? What do they care about? Give them their own story.

SHARE YOUR SIX WORD WONDERS

Letting others see your work helps you improve. Don't be shy!

Go back through the workbook and choose your top six Six Word Wonders. **Now, share them with a loved one.** Someone you trust. **Ask for feedback. Look for ways to improve.**

Once you're happy with your wonders, why not enter them in the **Six Word Wonder Contest?** More details at the back of this book.

SIX WORD WONDER WORKBOOK CONCLUSION

I hope you've enjoyed this journey into the creation process for a Six Word Wonder.

Keep writing. **Practice is the best way to improve**, and as the saying goes, rest is rust.

Don't forget to consider the type of Six Word Wonder - is it a joke, a memoir, advice, a poem, or a story? What genre are you writing in? Then consider the different power verbs, curious nouns, punctation choices you can play with.

Lastly, be sure to refine and edit your story, and then share it!

BONUS: SIX WORD WONDER GENERATOR

On my website, **I built a fun little Six Word Wonder generator.** It uses a standard sentence order to create stories. It's also a useful exercise for understanding the structural elements of an English language sentence.

The word order of every story from the Six Word Wonder generator is Adjective, Noun, Adverb, Verb, Determiner, Noun.

Some stories generated are nonsense, some are downright bizarre. But others produce a kind of mad genius.

Here are some examples of stories the generator has offered up:

Painful pig candidly phoned the snail.

Joyous Diane sedately felt the pencil.

Gloomy grandmother loyally trimmed the giraffe.

Sophisticated shark completely deceived the panther.

Evil scorpion yearningly observed the woman.

Drowsy Jacob bewilderingly pickled the lion.

Voiceless elephant grudgingly talked the bones.

Mercurial dentist wonderfully scolded the kid.

Shrill Amy properly smelt the professor.

Tame goat successfully relaxed the uncle.

Why not make some of your own?

Visit dougweller.net/generator to play with the generator.

BONUS: PLAY THE SIX WORD WONDER GAME

The Six Word Wonder Game is a fun game for all ages, for two to eight players. In the game, players must think of famous people and places, and describe them in only six words.

Six Word Wonder Game Rules

Objective:

The object of the game is to **earn points by guessing the most correct answers to six word clues** given by your opponents.

Equipment required:

You do not need any equipment to play other than your general knowledge, although you may want a pen and paper to keep score.

Game Play:

The game consists of **four rounds: Celebrity, Historical Figure, Famous Landmarks, Other Players.**

In the first round, the first player becomes the Describer. They must **think of a Celebrity, then describe them to the other players using only six words.** When another player guesses the correct answer, both the Describer and the correct player receive five points. **If any Describer uses more than six words in their description, or accidentally says the name of the Celebrity they are describing, they lose ten points.** If no player is able to guess the correct answer, the Describer must end their turn.

Going clockwise, the next player now thinks of a different celebrity to describe using six words, and all the other players try to guess. Again, whoever guesses the correct answer first wins five points. The round ends when every player has described one celebrity.

The winner of the first round starts the second round. The same rules apply, except this time the player must describe a Historical Figure to the other players.

At the end of the second round, the winner starts the third round, this time on Famous Landmarks. The final round requires every player in turn to think of one of the other players, and then use six words to describe them. In a two-player game, choose a person both players know.

Winner: At the end of the final round, **whoever has earned the most points wins.** In the event of a tie between two or more players, whichever player won the most rounds wins.

THANK YOU, YOU CLEVER, CLEVER THING

I've been writing Six Word Wonders for many years now. If ever I'm struggling with writer's block, or needing a quick blast of creativity, six words is my go to solution.

From the blank page challenge of creation to the process of whittling the words down to their most efficient and effective form, I can't resist.

Since I started sharing these micro-fictions, I've discovered communities of people who love this tiny art form. And I've encountered others, of course, who loathe this genre. Some demand that the a Six Word Wonder "must tell a story", others are frustrated that the form offers only a fragment of a bigger story. But while I continue to find the form freeing and surprising, I will continue. There is probably no perfect six word story out there. But I will keep trying to get closer to discovering it.

A few personal thanks:

First, to my wife, Kirsty, who shared my quarantine as we both battled Covid during the writing of this book. I love you. Also, all thanks to my loving family, scattered across the world. Especially my wonderful parents, Avril and Denis, who gave me this love of language and a warped sense of humour. The cats and dogs we fostered and cared for during the book writing progress were: Scampy, Sammy, Alan, Simon, and Zoe. We support a charity called the Stray Cat Alliance. They have a 'no kill' policy, saving cats lives every day.

Thank you all my beta and ARC readers, with special thanks to Colin Parfitt. If you are interested in being a beta reader or receiving an advance reader copy for future books, then simply join the mailing list at dougweller.net

Most of all, I would like to once again thank everybody who entered the Six Word Wonder contest. It gave me so much joy to read and share your stories. I hope you keep writing your Six Word Wonders.

Lastly, thank you for reading Six Word Stories. If you enjoyed the book, you can let me know by leaving a review on Goodreads or Amazon.

Final thought, till next we meet:

Enjoy your life. There's no repeat.

SIX WORD WONDER 2022
SHORTLIST

Below is the complete rundown of shortlisted writers for the Six Word Wonder contest.

Abbie Harris, United Kingdom
Alan Russell, United Kingdom
Alice Raison, United Kingdom
Alison McBain, United States
Aliyaa Pathan, United States
Alyanna Sy, Philippines
Ambar Marrero, United States
Amy Cree, United States
Ane Garalde, Canada
Angela Deane, United Kingdom
Anna Scaife, New Zealand
Annmarie Ragukonis, United States
Kiera Gracie

Ashley Gilland, United States
Ashley Gonzales
Awneet Singh, India
Bethany Jarmul
Bradley Sancken, Japan
Brea Pringle, Australia
Brian Hall, Australia
Carmen Bock
Casey Curtis, United States
Chris Clemens, Canada
Christopher Witty, France
Clarissa Mchardy, United Kingdom
Danielle Hall, United States
David Silver, United Kingdom
Desirel Ng, Australia
Diana Davison, Australia
Dj Robbins
Donald A. Ranard, United States
Donald W. Falconer
Ebony Bell, Australia
Elisa Gabrielle Donahue, United States
Emily Delforce, Australia
Emma Hartley, United States
Emma Moisa, Netherlands
Erin P McCurdy, United States
Fiona Grainger, United Kingdom
Georgia Lewis, Australia

Gordon Langley
Granville Brown, United Kingdom
Hans van Weerd, Australia
Heather Gillespie, Canada
Heather Wightman, United Kingdom
Humna Khan, Australia
Ian Davos, Romania
Jake Findlay, United Kingdom
James A. Tweedie, United States
James Michelle, United States
Jan Price, United Kingdom
Jeff Kennedy, Anguilla
Jennifer Haggerty, United States
Jennifer McCubbin, United States
Jeremy Delgado, United States
Jillian Lennon
Jo Mularczyk, Australia
Joann Majerle, United States
John Morris, United Kingdom
John Pearce, Australia
Jon Colman, United Kingdom
Jude Abraham, Israel
Jules Martin, United States
Juliana Ghetto, Australia
Julie Bobzien, United States
Julie McNeely-Kirwan, United States
Katy Deland, United States

Katie Ulrich, United States
Krash Blamdicute, United States
Kyla Gruta, Philippines
Kyriakos Chalkopoulos, Greece
La-Chanda Smith, United States
Laura Beck, United States
L. E. Morgan, Australia
Leena Knell Nox, Australia
Leslie Roberts, United Kingdom
Lily Murphy, Australia
Lin Let, United Kingdom
Lisa Marie Lopez
Lottie Dale, United Kingdom
Luke Shepherd
Mackenzie Stoudt, United States
Manesh Koshy George, India
Martha Letseka, Lesotho
Martin Cameron, United Kingdom
Matthew Ochrym, United States
Matthew Rowe, United Kingdom
Maureen Crisp, United Kingdom
Megan Oliver, Australia
Michael P. Aleman, United States
Michelle Keeley, United Kingdom
Mike Walker
Miriam Ikwueme, Nigeria
Monica Fernandez, United States

Natasia Rea, United States
Nicky Cassar White, Malta
O'Neill Renton, United Kingdom
Olivia Hartwell, United Kingdom
Olivia Lindquist
Olivine Marie, United States
Padma Poorani S, India
Paul Lewthwaite, United Kingdom
Paul Toolan
Petra Glover
Phanindra Ivatury, Netherlands
Philip Kingsley, United Kingdom
Philomena Daly, Ireland
Pragya P, India
Princes Rose Manuel, Philippines
Rashi Gaikwad, India
Rebekah Lawrence, United Kingdom
Rhonda Russell
Richard Liu, Taiwan
Richard Salsbury, United Kingdom
Robert Carroll, United States
Rohith Bandaratilaka, Sri Lanka
Royston Ellis, Sri Lanka
Bligh Chanan-Turner, Australia
Ruth Jepson, United Kingdom
Sagar J, India
Sam Mitchell, United Kingdom

Samuel Chrapot, Australia

Scott Bradbrook

Sean Wright, United States

Sebya Gorre-Clancy, United States

Shaun McKenna, United Kingdom

Siraj Khan, United States

Skylar Peck, South Korea

Sneha Mukherjee,

Sneha Shree Saikia, India

Soft Remedy, Indonesia

Stuart McDowall, United Kingdom

Sue Mitchell, Australia

Summer Austin, United States

Tamsin Kerr, Australia

Tarrah Cheramie

Tashi Chaturvedi, India

Thomas Stewart, United States

Tim Kirton

Torché Johnson, United States

Wendy Eisenberg, United States

Xan Indigo, France

Yess Bryce

ALSO AVAILABLE BY DOUG WELLER

The Six Word Wonder series:

Six Word Wonder

Six Word Story

Six Word Wonder Workbook

For Adults:

The Forgetting Cycle

For Yonger Readers

Calico Rae - The Twisted Towers (coming June 2022)

Boy In A Box (coming September 2022)

Doug Weller is a story writer and the brain behind the
Six Word Wonder.

THINK THIS IS EASY? PROVE IT!

We are running a writing contest to find the next great stories, memoirs, poems, memoirs, and jokes.

One Six Word Wonder chosen by the judges will:

- Be crowned Six Word Wonder winner
- Get published in the next book in the Six Word Wonder series
- Win $100

Shortlisted writers may also be published in the next book in the Six Word Wonder series. To enter the contest, visit:

dougweller.net/contest

Printed in Great Britain
by Amazon